POKÉMON®

Catch That Wobbuffet!

Adapted by
Tracey West

SCHOLASTIC INC.
New York   Toronto   London   Auckland   Sydney
Mexico City   New Delhi   Hong Kong   Buenos Aires

OFFICIAL
POKÉMON
MASTER'S
CLUB

Published by Scholastic Inc.
90 Old Sherman Turnpike, Danbury, CT 06816.

SCHOLASTIC and associated logos are trademarks and/or registered trademarks of Scholastic Inc.

ISBN 0-439-72203-9

First Scholastic Printing, September 2005

Ash and his friends Brock and Misty were walking in the woods. *"Pika?"* said Pikachu. It saw something on the path.

Two strange people stopped them. "This is our new PokéPod," said one. "We want to try it out. We'll use Pikachu."

The strange people took
Pikachu. They put Pikachu
in the PokéPod.

Then they took
off their glasses
and coats.
"Team Rocket!"
Ash cried.

"We tricked
you," said
Jessie. "Now we
have your
Pikachu!" said
James.
Team Rocket
ran off with Pikachu.

Team Rocket had a plan.
Jessie gave Pikachu to her
Wobbuffet.
Then Wobbuffet ran away.

But Wobbuffet fell into the river.
The blue Pokémon dropped Pikachu.

Ash caught Pikachu just in time.
"Now open this PokéPod right now!"
Ash told Team Rocket.

"The PokéPod will not open without a key," Jessie said.

"Then give me the key," Ash said.

"We don't have it" said Jessie. "We gave it to Wobbuffet."

"Catch that Wobbuffet!" Ash cried.
Wobbuffet floated down the river.
Ash and his friends ran after
Wobbuffet.

Team Rocket chased the Psychic
Pokémon, too.

Just then, *thump!* Wobbuffet
bumped into a Quagsire.
  "*Quagsire,*" said the Water
Pokémon. Quagsire showed
Wobbuffet how to get to land.

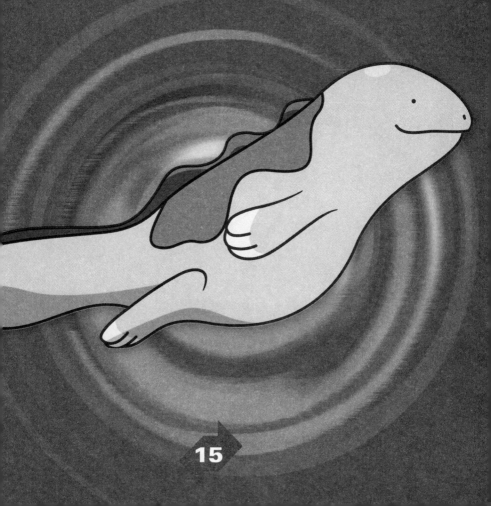

Wobbuffet got out of the water. It climbed up a tree. It grabbed a vine and swung from tree to tree.

Everyone chased Wobbuffet
through the woods. They ran
down a hill.

"Where is Wobbuffet?"
Ash asked.

"Wobbuffet is up there!" Jessie cried, pointing.

A tree branch stuck out of the hill. Poor Wobbuffet was hanging from the branch.

Zoom! A truck came speeding down the road.

Wobbuffet fell. It landed on the truck.

Then Officer Jenny drove up. "Step aside," she said. "We have to catch that truck!"

"A thief named Goneff is in that truck," Officer Jenny said.

"We have to catch the truck, too," Ash said. He told her about Wobbuffet.

"Get in fast!" Officer Jenny said.

Ash and his friends got into the police car.

The police caught up to Goneff.

"I will get away in my balloon!" cried Goneff.

But Wobbuffet got into the balloon first! Everyone watched Wobbuffet fly away.

Team Rocket got into their balloon.
They chased after Wobbuffet.
Wobbuffet tried to jump into the
balloon. But Wobbuffet broke the
balloon by mistake!

Wobbuffet fell to the ground.

Ash called on his Chikorita. "Chikorita, use Vine Whip to catch Wobbuffet!" he cried.

23 ➡

Chikorita grabbed Wobbuffet with its vines.

Wobbuffet landed in a speedboat. The boat zoomed down the river.

Ash ran down one side of
the river.

Team Rocket ran down the
other side of the river.

Then Ash and Jessie jumped
into the speeding boat.

Ash and Jessie could not stop
Wobbuffet's boat.
Wobbuffet flew out of the boat.
"Come back, Wobbuffet!"
Jessie yelled.

The boat was about to crash into a bridge.

"Totodile, I choose you!" Ash yelled.

Totodile used Water Gun to slow down the boat.

Ash and Jessie landed safely.
Officer Jenny ran up to Ash.
"Goneff the thief got away
again," she said. "He is in that old
building. And Wobbuffet is with him!"

Inside the building, Goneff
and Wobbuffet were not alone.
Goneff called on his Golem,
a super-tough Rock Pokémon.

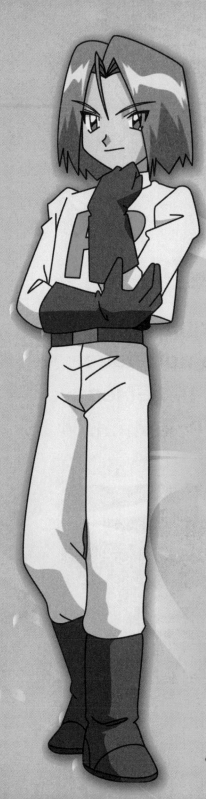

Team Rocket dug a tunnel. They got into the building.

"Hand over that Wobbuffet!" James told Goneff.

"Golem, go get them!" Goneff yelled.

Ash and Totodile ran through the tunnel.

Ash saw Golem attacking Team Rocket.

Totodile blasted Golem with Water Gun.

Golem fought back.

Golem tried to tackle Totodile.

But Wobbuffet used a move called Counter.

Golem and Goneff crashed through the wall.

"We have you now!" Officer Jenny told them.

But Team Rocket took off with
Wobbuffet in a new balloon.
"Oh no!" Ash cried. "Wobbuffet
still has the key!"
"*Pika!*" said Pikachu.

Ash called on his Noctowl. "Peck a hole in that balloon!" he cried.

Noctowl pecked away. Air shot out of the balloon.

The key fell from Wobbuffet's neck. It landed in Ash's hand.

Ash got Pikachu out of the PokéPod.

"Pika . . . chuuu!" Pikachu hit Team Rocket with Thunderbolt.

"Team Rocket's blasting off again!" they wailed.

"Thank you for helping us catch the thief," Officer Jenny told Ash.

"We are just happy that Pikachu is out of that PokéPod," Ash said. Misty and Brock hugged Pikachu.

"Pika! Pika!" Pikachu agreed.

Who's That Psychic Pokémon?

37

See page 45 or your
Psychic Pokédex for the answer.

Psychic Eyes

Can you tell who these Psychic Pokémon are by just looking at each one's eyes?

Check page 45, your *Ultimate Sticker Book*, or your *Psychic Pokédex* for the answers.

Battle Time!

Now it is your turn to battle! Read about each battle below. Then pick the best Pokémon to use against your opponent. In each battle, all of the Pokémon are the same level.

1. Here comes Machop, a skilled Fighting Pokémon. Which of these Pokémon has the best chance to beat this Fighting Pokémon?

| Grumpig™ | Glalie™ | Nosepass™ |
| (Psychic) | (Ice) | (Rock) |

2. Your opponent brings out Ralts to battle you. Which of these Pokémon can best stand up to its Psychic attacks?

Nidorino™
(Poison)

Mankey™
(Fighting)

Mawile™
(Steel)

3. Watch out! A sizzling Pikachu has entered the battle. Which of these Pokémon will last the longest against this Electric Type?

Squirtle™
(Water)

Cubone™
(Ground)

Taillow™
(Normal/Flying)

41

Check page 45 or your *Pokédex* books for the answers.

Know Your Legends

Three Psychic Pokémon are pictured in each row. One of them is Legendary. Can you pick out the Legendary Pokémon in each row?

1. Latias™   Xatu™   Girafarig™

2. Mewtwo™   Espeon™   Abra™

3. Deoxys™   Mr. Mime™   Gardevoir™

4. Natu™   Lunatone™   Lugia™

5. Smoochum™   Jirachi™   Meditite™

6. Alakazam™   Celebi™   Starmie™

7. Slowking™   Beldum™   Mew™

Check page 45 or your *Psychic Pokédex* for the answers.

Psychic Pokémon Jokes

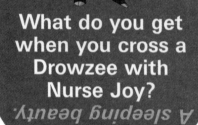

What do you get when you cross a Drowzee with Nurse Joy?

A sleeping beauty.

What happened to the Exeggcute when it laughed?

It cracked up.

How can you tell if Lugia is hiding under your bed?

Because your nose touches the ceiling!

Why couldn't the Psychic Pokémon play basketball?

Because its crystal ball kept breaking!

Why did the boy run away from the girl Pokémon trainer?

Because she said she wanted a Smoochum!

Knock knock!
Who's there?
Wy?
Wy who?
Wynaut become a Psychic Pokémon Trainer?

Answers

Page 37: Who's That Psychic Pokémon?
Wynaut!

Pages 38-39: Psychic Eyes
1. Ralts
2. Jirachi
3. Spoink
4. Chimecho
5. Mr. Mime
6. Wobbuffet
7. Smoochum
8. Solrock

Pages 40-41: Battle Time!
1. Grumpig (Psychic beats Fighting)
2. Mawile (Steel beats Psychic)
3. Cubone (Ground beats Electric)

Pages 42-43: Know Your Legends
1. Latias
2. Mewtwo
3. Deoxys
4. Lugia
5. Jirachi
6. Celebi
7. Mew